OWL IN THE HOUSE

Gregory Evans • Peter Bailey

BLue Bananas

To Daniel and Isobel
G.E.

For Ella
P.B.

Gregory Evans • Peter Bailey

MAMMOTH

First published in Great Britain 1997 by Mammoth
an imprint of Egmont Children's Books Limited
Michelin House, 81 Fulham Rd, London SW3 6RB.
Published in hardback by Heinemann Library,
a division of Reed Educational and Professional Publishing Limited
by arrangement with Egmont Children's Books Limited.

This edition produced for The Book People Ltd
Hall Wood Avenue, Haydock, St Helens, WA11 9UL

Text copyright © Greg Evans 1997
Illustrations © Peter Bailey 1997
The Author and Illustrator have asserted their moral rights.
Paperback ISBN 0 7497 2633 4
Hardback ISBN 0 434 97654 7
10 9 8 7 6 5
A CIP catalogue record for this title is available from the British Library.
Printed at Oriental Press Limited, Dubai.

Owl's first hunting trip was not going well.

Before Owl could catch anything,

a storm blew up. Clouds hid the moon.

Rain poured down.

The wind was fierce.

What a night!

Owl was blown to the top of an old beech tree. The tree tossed and swayed. Owl clung on tightly, looking for somewhere to shelter.

Then Owl saw the house.

One lighted window hung in the

dark like the last golden leaf on an

autumn tree.

A little girl, woken by the storm,
was getting a drink of water.

Owl flew through the rainy night

and landed on the chimney pot.

A sudden gust of wind made Owl lose his balance and tumble into the chimney.

Owl felt frightened, but the house
was warm and calm after the stormy
night. He shook his sooty feathers
and flew off.

13

In the hall, Owl stood still and spread his wings. No wind ruffled his feathers. There were no smells of trees or grass, earth or rain. So Owl knew the house was locked up tight, like a big sealed box.

How can I get out?

Owl found a little animal in a cage.

'Who are you?' asked Owl.

'I'm a gerbil,' the animal replied,

keeping well away from Owl's claws.

16

'The wind blew me down your chimney
and now I can't get out. Can you tell
me how to get free?' asked Owl.

17

'Free?' said the gerbil. 'You don't want

to be free. You want to be safe.'

'What's safe?' asked Owl.

'I'm safe,' said the gerbil. 'Safe in this

cage, where no one can harm me.

If I wasn't in here, you'd eat me,

wouldn't you?'

'No,' Owl said, truthfully. 'You're too

big. You'd put up too much of a fight.'

Owl spread his wings and flew off, leaving the gerbil safe behind the bars of her cage.

In the kitchen, a dog snored softly in a basket. Owl perched on a chair and cleared his throat.

The dog opened his eyes. 'An owl!'

he said. 'What are you doing here?'

'The wind blew me down your chimney,'

said Owl, 'and now I can't get out. Can

you tell me how to get free?'

The dog yawned.

'You don't want to be free,' said the dog.

'You want to be cared for.'

'What's cared for?' asked Owl.

'I'm cared for. By the little girl.

She strokes me and takes me for a walk.

She gives me biscuits.'

Owl ate a biscuit.

It had a dry, fishy taste.

Not as good as beetle, but not bad.

'May I have another?' Owl asked.

He was very hungry.

'Have them all,' said the dog.

When the dish was empty, Owl wiped
his beak on his wing.

'Thank you,' he said.

'Don't thank me,' said the dog. 'Those
were the cat's.' Then he shut his eyes
and began to snore.

Upstairs, the little girl sat up in bed. The storm was quiet now, but she still couldn't sleep. She held the torch she used for reading under the covers.

As Owl flew into her room, the little
girl clicked on her torch.

In its beam, Owl's eyes shone

like jewels.

'Please help me,' asked Owl. 'The wind blew me down the chimney and I can't get out. How can I get free?'

'You don't want to be free,' said the

little girl. 'You want to be loved.'

'What's loved?' asked Owl.

The girl stroked Owl gently.

'I'll love you,' she said softly. 'I'll keep

you safe like my gerbil. I'll care for you

like my dog and my cat.'

'I'll make you mine,' said the little girl.
'You'll have your own cosy box. I'll find
you beetles. I'll take you to the field
and let you fly. But you must come
back. Will you promise
to come back?'

Owl was silent. He seemed to have

fallen asleep.

Owl was about to promise, when he heard a noise from downstairs, like a small door opening and closing.

A breath of wind touched his feathers. It smelled of outside, of woods and streams, earth and grass.

Without looking back,

Owl flew out of the bedroom and

followed the thin trail of scent.

In the kitchen, the dog was still asleep in his basket.

A young tabby cat was drinking milk from a saucer. Her sleek damp fur smelled of outside. Of freedom.

The cat lapped up the last drop of milk
and looked at Owl.

'Did you eat my biscuits?' the cat said.

'The dog said I could,' Owl explained.

'He didn't tell me they were yours

until I'd eaten them all.'

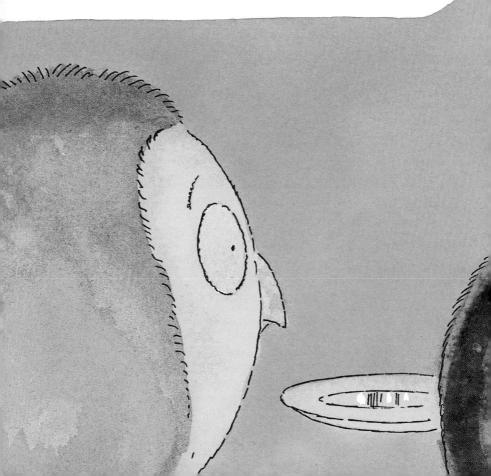

'Typical,' said the cat. 'Never mind.

I had a fieldmouse while I was out.'

'Out?' said Owl. 'You've been out?'

'Naturally,' said the cat.

'Then can you tell me how to get free?'

The cat nodded towards the door to the garden.

For the first time, Owl saw another little door set into it, close to the floor.

'My own private entrance,' said the cat, with pride. 'But I'll let you use it. Just this once.'

Owl looked through the little door. The storm had passed and the night was calm and clear. The moon was bright, sailing above the clouds. Owl knew the hunting would be good.

Owl pushed through the cat-flap
and out of the house.

Then he flew away into the beautiful
freedom of the night.

But the cat wasn't listening.

She was too busy eating the dish of dog

biscuits she had found under the table.

'Please say goodbye to the gerbil and the dog and the little girl,' Owl said to the cat. 'Especially the little girl.'